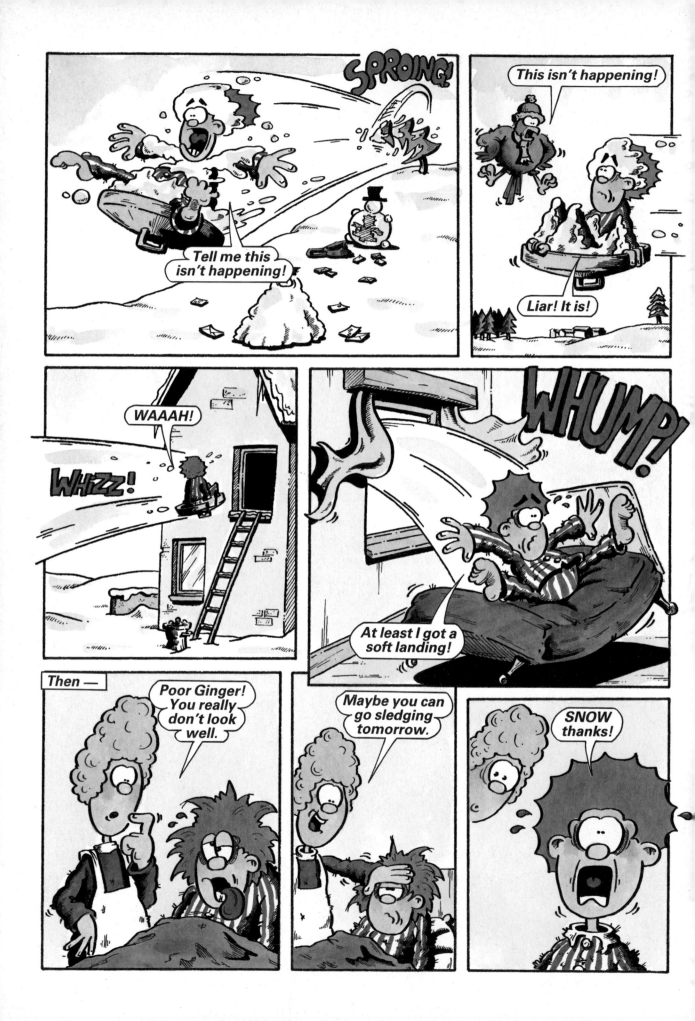

Baby Crockett's WINTER Diary —

Me likes Winter speshly if it SNOWS!

Me can roll big snowballs

and make a snowman

Dad not to happy when he found out me used his clothes for my snowman

Me got plenty of 'ammo' for Willum when he comes in

But he surpised me wiv a big snowball

Me was frozen

So me went into the house to thaw out

Next day me go out to get Willum wiv a big snowball

But all the snow had melted even my big snowman was like a snow mouse

have to think of something to get even on willum

Baby Crockett

new years eve

Mum says at New Year you make out a List of fings You will do better next year. This is called making your rezton Revoloshuns Rezshun doing things better next year. Here is my LIST....